Tracee Bennett

Bonnie Pryor

GRANDPA BEAR

Illustrated by Bruce Degen

William Morrow & Company, Inc., New York

Library of Congress Cataloging in Publication Data: Pryor, Bonnie. Grandpa Bear. Summary: Four episodes demonstrate the imaginative games Grandpa Bear plays with Samantha and the affection between them. 1. Children's stories, American. [1. Grandfathers—Fiction. 2. Bears—Fiction. 3. Imagination—Fiction] I. Degen, Bruce, ill. II. Title. PZ7.P94965Gr 1985 [E] 84-25545 ISBN 0-688-04551-0 | ISBN 0-688-04552-9 (lib. bdg.)

To Tracee Bennett
Love from Grandpa Bear
and
Bonnie Pryor

To Bob, who gave me the time
B.P.

For Elizabeth Jordan
B.D.

"I am getting old," said Grandpa Bear. "My bones
creak, my ears are tired, and my eyes cannot see far."

"Come and live with us," said Mama Bear. "You
can sit on the porch and watch the days go by."

So Grandpa Bear came to live at Samantha's
house.

One day Samantha's big brother, Harry Bear, was
getting ready to go to town with his friends.

"I want to go, too," said Samantha.

"No," said Mama Bear. "You are too little."

Mama Bear sat in the chair and rocked Baby
Bear. Samantha played with her blocks by herself.
She felt very cross.

"I have always wanted to go to the moon," said Grandpa Bear. "But it would be very lonely to go by myself. Will you help me build a rocket?"

"I want to come, too," said Harry Bear. "No," said Grandpa Bear. "You are too big. And Baby Bear is too small. But Samantha is just right."

Samantha and Grandpa Bear found some boxes. They made a rocket. They made it strong enough to go to the moon.

"Will you be gone very long?" asked Mama Bear.

"Maybe yes and maybe no," said Grandpa Bear. "It is a long way to the moon."

Mama Bear made them each a sandwich and put them in a sack. Then she put in two apples.

"Now you will not be hungry on the moon," she said.

"Wait," said Grandpa Bear. "It is a very long way to the moon. We will need some cake for such a long trip."

Mama Bear gave them each a big piece of cake to take to the moon.

"Now we are ready," said Grandpa Bear. They climbed into the rocket. Soon they were far from home.

"Oh, dear," said Grandpa Bear. "I have forgotten my glasses. Now how can I see the moon?"

"Don't worry, Grandpa," Samantha said. "I will tell you what I see."

"It was lucky for me you came along," said Grandpa Bear. "Can you see the moon?"

"Not yet," said Samantha. "But I see our home far away."

"I am very hungry," said Grandpa Bear. "I think we should eat our cake. On the way to the moon you can eat your cake first."

They ate all the cake.

"Now can you see the moon?" asked Grandpa Bear.

"Not yet," said Samantha. "But it is very dark, and the sky is full of stars."

"Riding in rockets is hard on my bones," said Grandpa Bear. "I hope we get there soon."

"We are almost there," Samantha said. "I can see the moon very near. It is big and round."

When the rocket landed, Samantha and Grandpa Bear climbed out.

"What do you see?" asked Grandpa Bear.

"I see rocks and hills," said Samantha. "And I see some moon men. They look very hungry."

"It's a good thing we still have our apples," said Grandpa Bear. They shared the apples with the moon men.

"The moon men still look hungry," said Samantha. "Maybe we had better give them our sandwiches."

The moon men ate all the sandwiches. They looked very happy.

"The moon men are very nice," said Samantha. "But I miss Mama Bear and Baby Bear."

"I think we should go home," said Grandpa Bear. "I can smell dinner cooking."

They waved good-bye to the moon men and climbed back into the rocket.

"How can you smell dinner cooking so far away on the earth?" asked Samantha.

"Oh," said Grandpa Bear. "My eyes are not good. My ears are not good. But my nose is very good."

"Why do you have so many wrinkles, Grandpa Bear?" asked Samantha.

"It is because I am old," said Grandpa Bear. "I have one wrinkle for every year I have lived."

"Were there dinosaurs when you were young?" asked Samantha.

"Let me see," said Grandpa Bear. "It is hard to remember so long ago. But I do seem to remember something about them."

"Tell me a story about them," begged Samantha.

Grandpa Bear sat in his chair. He rocked, and he thought.

"Well," said Grandpa Bear. "A long time ago, I was little like you."

"Did you have a mother?" asked Samantha.

"Yes," said Grandpa Bear. "And a father and sister and brother."

"One day my sister went to play with her friends. But I could not go because I was too little. My mother rocked the baby in her arms, but I was too big."

"What did you do?" asked Samantha.

"I was very cross," said Grandpa. "I played by myself in my yard. That was when I saw it."

"What did you see?" asked Samantha.

"It was a dinosaur coming right toward our house. He was very big and green. He had sharp teeth and breathed fire out of his nose."

"That must have been a dragon," said Samantha.
"Dragons breathe fire from their mouth."

"You may be right," said Grandpa Bear. "Now
that I think of it, it was a dragon."

"What did it do?" asked Samantha.

"The dragon was coming right to our house.
Clump! Clump! I could see it coming closer and
closer. Sometimes it stopped to eat up a tree."

"I didn't know dragons ate trees," Samantha said.

"This one did," said Grandpa Bear. "This one ate everything."

"What did you do?" asked Samantha.

"Wait," said Grandpa Bear. "I am trying to remember."

He thought for a long time.

"I remember," said Grandpa Bear. "I was very angry. The dragon was making a terrible mess. He was stepping on houses and knocking down trees. 'Stop,' I said. And I stepped on his tail."

"Did that make the dragon angry?" asked Samantha.

"Oh, no." said Grandpa Bear. "He started to cry. He was a terrible baby. But his tears were so big that soon everything was covered with water. I had to do something quick before our house turned into a lake."

14

"What did you do then?" Samantha asked.

"There was only one thing left to do," said Grandpa Bear. "I picked up my rope and lassoed that dragon. I took him all the way to China and turned him loose. A lot of dragons live in China. The dragon was very happy to see his friends."

"Were you scared?" Samantha asked.

"Oh, yes," said Grandpa Bear. "That was the day I got my first wrinkle."

16

Three

Samantha came home from school. Grandpa Bear was on the porch. He was rocking in his chair, and his eyes were closed.

"Are you asleep?" asked Samantha.

"No," said Grandpa Bear. "I am watching my garden grow."

"I don't see any garden," said Samantha.

"That is because your eyes are open," said Grandpa Bear. "Come and sit beside me and close your eyes. Now can you see it?"

"Yes," said Samantha. "I can see it now. I can see tulips and roses."

"Can you see marigolds and petunias?" asked Grandpa Bear.

"Yes," said Samantha. "I can see them."

Harry Bear came out on the porch.

"What are you doing?" he asked.

"We are watching our garden grow," said Samantha.

"I do not see a garden," said her brother. "I only see cars and a road."

"Close your eyes," said Samantha. "Now do you see it?"

"No," said Harry Bear. "I am too old."

"Maybe you are not old enough," said Grandpa.

The next day Samantha and Grandpa Bear
walked to the store. They bought some seeds and a
flowerpot. They put dirt in the pot and planted the
seeds. Then they watered the seeds and put them
in the sun to grow. In time the pot was full of
flowers.

"I like the flowers," said Harry Bear. "But I wish there were more. I wish there were a hundred flowers growing."

"Close your eyes," said Grandpa Bear. "Can you see them now?"

"Yes," said Harry Bear. "I do see them. I can see roses and tulips."

"Can you see marigolds and petunias?" asked Samantha.

"Yes," said Harry Bear. "I can see them now."

They sat on the porch watching the flowers grow until Mama Bear called them all in for dinner.

Four

All of Harry Bear's friends came for a visit. They played music and danced. Samantha peeked in.

"Can I dance with you?" she asked.

"Go away," said her brother. "You are too little."

Samantha went to her room. She got out her blocks and made a tower. It was a tall tower. It was the best tower she had ever made.

"See my tower, Baby Bear," she said.

Baby Bear knocked down the tower. The blocks went all over the floor. Samantha was very angry. She hit Baby Bear and made him cry.

"Baby Bear is very little," said Mama Bear. "He does not know any better. But you are old enough to know you should not hit the baby."

Mama Bear was very upset. She sent Samantha to bed.

Samantha picked up her blocks and put them away. She climbed into bed.

Just then Grandpa Bear came into the room.

"Mama Bear is very cross," he said. "She said you could not have a bedtime story. But she did not say you could not tell me a story. Will you tell me a story?"

"I don't know any stories," said Samantha.

"You think," said Grandpa Bear. "I will wait until you can think of a story to tell me."

"I know a story," said Samantha.

"Good," said Grandpa Bear. "I am listening."

"Once upon a time there was a little bear. She was too little to do the things her brother could do. She was too big to do the things the baby bear could do. Then one day her grandpa came. She was just the right size to do the things her grandpa could do.

"The end."

Samantha looked at her grandpa.

"Did you like my story?" she asked.

But Grandpa Bear did not answer. He was sound asleep.